1987 39

This book belongs to

____

Published by Toy Works Press
902 Broadway, New York, New York 10010

Printed in Singapore

ISBN 0-938715-02-X

By Marcus Donnely
Illustrated by Debby Young

Like most little boys, William loved riding his tricycle and eating chocolate ice cream and splashing in puddles and all the other things little boys everywhere do. But the thing little William loved more than anything else in the world—even more than getting presents—was digging deep, deep holes in the ground in the woods near his house.

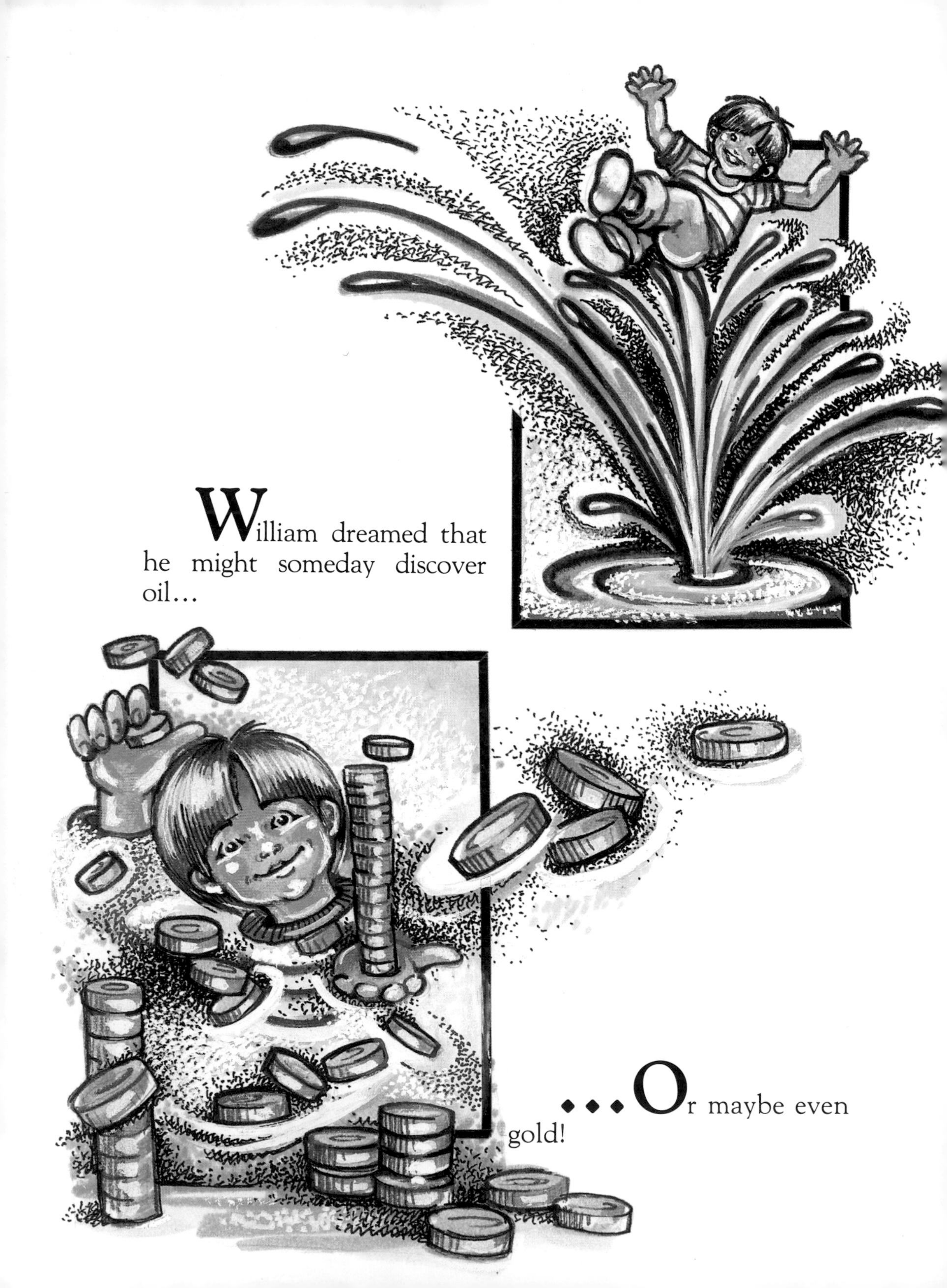

William dreamed that he might someday discover oil...

...Or maybe even gold!

But alas, all poor William ever discovered were a few old bottles, a broken clay pot, some rusty bedsprings and one Indian arrowhead.

Until one day, when William was digging at a place deeper and farther into the forest than he had ever been before, he discovered a great lopsided ball! Whatever in the world could it be? William wondered.

"Maybe it's a dinosaur egg," he laughed—for William knew that all the dinosaurs had disappeared from the earth millions of years before.

Even though William had no idea what it was, it was so smooth and shiny and pretty that he decided to take it home and put it beside the warm radiator next to his bed.

That night, when William's father came into his bedroom to tuck him into bed, he saw the lopsided ball beside the radiator and asked, "What's that, William?"

"It's a dinosaur egg, Dad," William answered.

William's Dad laughed as he shut the door, for he was a college professor and he knew very well that dinosaurs no longer existed.

In a few minutes William was fast asleep. He dreamed of the time millions of years ago when dinosaurs big as buildings roamed the world.

He dreamed of Stegosaurus, the armored dinosaur with a row of bony plates on his back, and of Triceratops, the horned dinosaur. He also dreamed of Tyrannosaurus, the two-legged, meat-eating dinosaur, and of Brontosaurus, the four-legged, plant-eating dinosaur who was more than seventy feet long and weighed thirty tons!

Some scientists said that dinosaurs no longer existed because once upon a time the earth erupted and covered all the grass and trees with ash and they had nothing to eat. And this made William very sad for dinosaurs.

The next morning William was awakened by a squeak. The first thing he saw when he looked over the edge of his bed was a cracked egg—and standing beside it, an animal such as he had never seen before! William was amazed. Could it be that his egg had hatched a baby dinosaur?

"Who—who are you?" William asked.

"Squeak," the tiny animal answered.

"Squeak . . ?" William repeated. He rather liked that name. Then he asked, "Are you a baby dinosaur?"

"Squeak, squeak," his little friend answered, nodding twice quickly.

Just then William's mother called from the hallway, "What's that squeaking?"

"Oh, just a dinosaur," William answered—which made his mother laugh.

William didn't really know for sure if Squeak was a dinosaur, a mouse or a rabbit—but he loved him just the same.

"From now on," William promised, "you'll be my pet dinosaur and I'll love you and take care of you forever."

"Squeak, squeak," his little pet dinosaur answered happily.

During the day, William was careful to hide Squeak from his parents.

But at night when he was alone in his room, William allowed Squeak to sleep in his bed with him.

When Squeak was big enough, he went with William into the forest, where he ate grass and leaves while William dug holes in the ground.

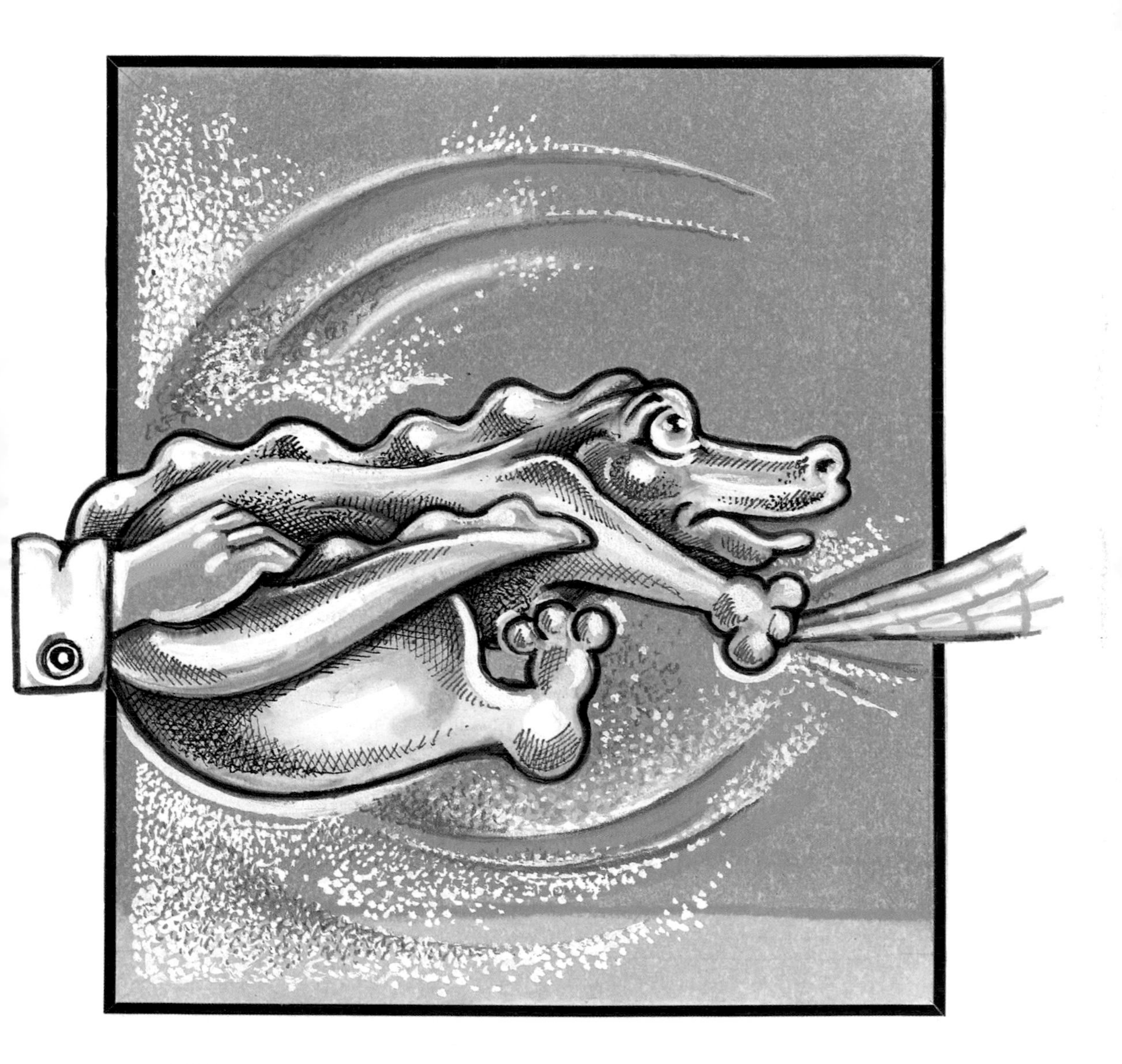

Each day Squeak grew bigger and bigger.
Until one day William's parents discovered him!
"Eek, a giant lizard!" William's mother screamed, while his father snatched poor Squeak out of bed by the tail.

"Pleasc don't hurt Squeak, Dad!" William cried. "He's my dinosaur."

"Dinosaur?" William's father asked—and Squeak nodded.

So William told his parents how he had dug up Squeak's egg and brought it home to hatch.

"He does look a *bit* like a dinosaur," William's father said, when William had finished. "But it's not possible," he added, "because dinosaurs became extinct millions of years ago."

But just to be sure, William's father called a paleontologist at the University where he taught...and the paleontologist called a biologist...and the biologist called still another scientist...

◆ ◆ ◆ And they all came to examine Squeak.

It might be a dinosaur, or it might be an unknown species of lizard, the scientists decided. They would have to take Squeak to their laboratory and run some tests to know for sure.

"What are you going to do to Squeak?" William cried.

"Don't worry, he'll be fine," the paleontologist promised.

"And you can visit him whenever you like," the biologist assured him.

For the next few days William was very lonely. And when he was finally allowed to visit Squeak, he was very sad at what he saw. Squeak was living in a cage that was much too small for him and he had instruments taped all over his body. William knew what he had to do.

"Don't worry, Squeak," William whispered, "I'm going to set you free."

"Squeak!" Squeak happily replied.

So on Sunday when all the scientists were at home, William sneaked into the laboratory...

...And set Squeak free!

They ran and ran—until they came to a place deeper into the forest than they had ever been before—a place where humans hardly ever came.

"This is where you'll live, Squeak," William told him. "I'm going to miss you, but you'll be safer here than you'll be with me. And besides, you're getting much too big to sleep in my bed anymore," William added, a little sad.

In fact Sqeak was much too big to even fit into William's bedroom anymore. And although Squeak knew he would miss William very much, he immediately felt much more at home in the forest than he ever had in a house.

"I'll visit you as often as I can," William promised, as Squeak gave him a great hug.

A dinosaur tear ran down Squeak's cheek as he watched his little friend disappear into the trees.

The next day, when the scientists discovered their dinosaur missing, they immediately set out to find him.

But of course they never did, because Squeak was much too wise to ever again be seen by anyone.

Except by William of course, who was always welcome.

As the years went by, William and Squeak both grew bigger and bigger.

And so did the tales of the large monster who lived in the forest. Some claimed he was an elephant who had escaped from the circus, while others, who swore they had seen him, claimed he was much too big to be an elephant.

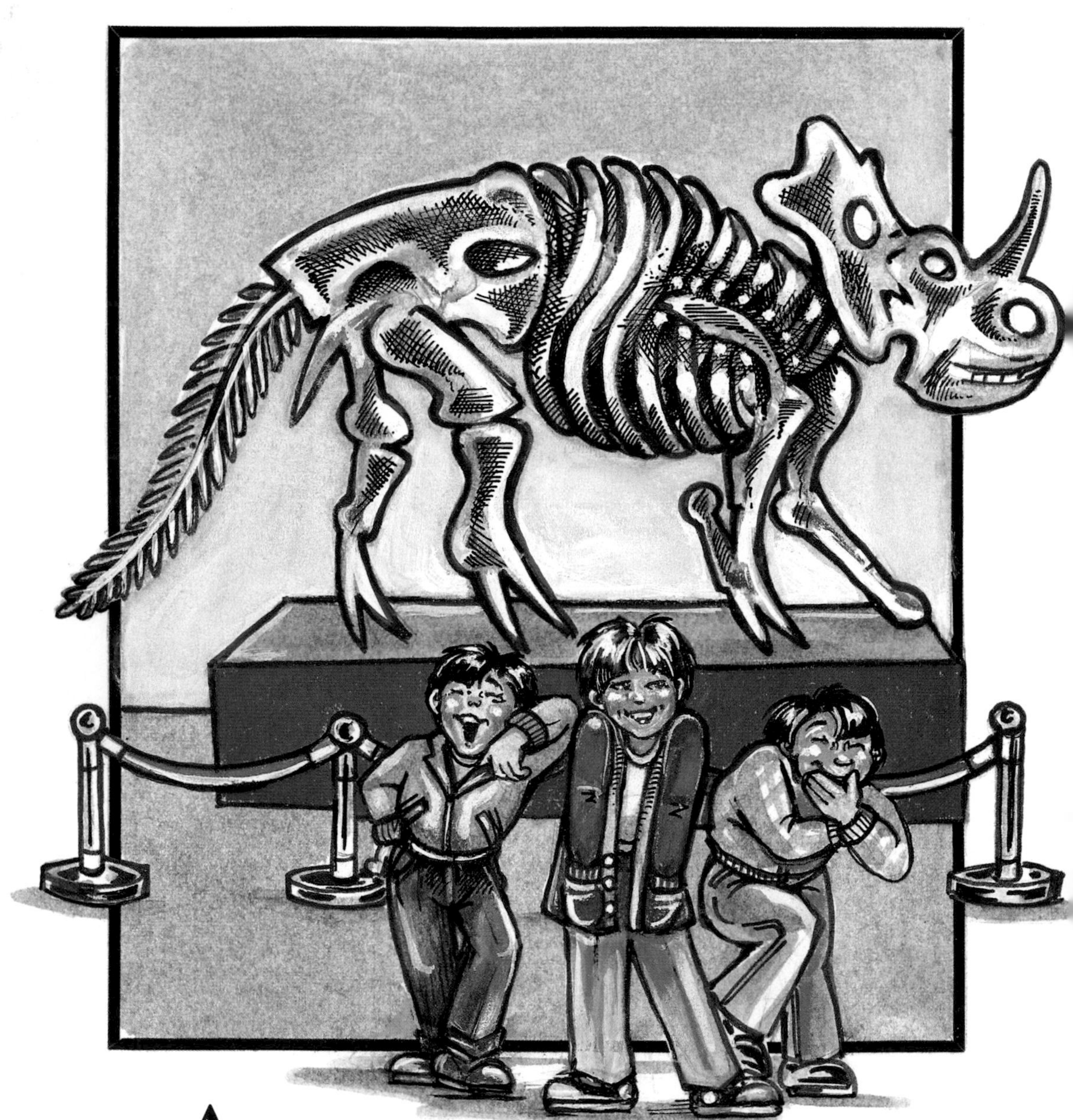

And when William suggested that he might be a dinosaur, everybody laughed—including William. For we all know that dinosaurs have been extinct for millions of years.

Don't we?